# Farmers

## A Level One Reader

By Cynthia Klingel and Robert B. Noyed

The Child's World®

When I grow up, I want to be a farmer.

A farmer gets up early in the morning.

A farmer goes to the barn to milk the cows.

A farmer feeds the pigs.

A farmer checks the chickens.

It is time to work in the fields.

A farmer uses big machines in the fields.

The fields are filled with different kinds of crops.

It is time to milk the cows again.

It has been a busy day.
I want to be a farmer!

# Word List

barn

crops

fields

tractors

# Note to Parents and Educators

Welcome to The Wonders of Reading™! These books provide text at three different levels for beginning readers to practice and strengthen their reading skills. In addition, the use of nonfiction text gives readers the valuable opportunity to *read to learn*, not just to learn to read.

These leveled readers allow children to choose books at their level of reading confidence and performance. Level One books offer beginning readers simple language, word choice, and sentence structure as well as a word list. Level Two books feature slightly more difficult vocabulary, longer sentences, and longer total text. In the back of each Level Two book are an index and a list of books and Web sites for finding out more information. Level Three books continue to extend word choice and length of text. In the back of each Level Three book are a glossary, an index, and a list of books and Web sites for further research.

State and national standards in reading and language arts emphasize using nonfiction at all levels of reading development. The Wonders of Reading™ books fill the historical void in nonfiction for primary grade readers with the additional benefit of a leveled text.

# About the Authors

Cynthia Klingel has worked as a high school English teacher and an elementary teacher. She is currently the curriculum director for a Minnesota school district. Writing children's books is another way for her to continue her passion for sharing the written word with children. Cynthia is a frequent visitor to the children's section of bookstores and enjoys spending time with her many friends, family, and two daughters.

Robert Noyed started his career as a newspaper reporter. Since then, he has worked in communications and public relations for more than fourteen years for a Minnesota school district. He enjoys writing books for children and finds that it brings a different feeling of challenge and accomplishment from other writing projects. He is an avid reader who also enjoys music, theater, traveling, and spending time with his wife, son, and daughter.

## Published by The Child's World®, Inc.
PO Box 326
Chanhassen, MN  55317-0326
800-599-READ
www.childsworld.com

**Photo Credits**
© 2002 Andy Sacks/Stone: 9
© 2002 Bruce Hands/Stone: cover
© 2002 Graeme Norways/Stone: 6
© 2002 Joel Larson/Stone: 18
© 2002 Jonathan Selig/Stone: 2
© 1993 Michael D. L. Jordan/Dembinsky Photo Assoc. Inc.: 21
© 2002 Mitch Kezar/Stone: 10
© Photri, Inc.: 17
© 2000 Richard Hamilton Smith/Dembinsky Photo Assoc. Inc.: 5, 13
© 2002 Zane Williams/Stone: 14

Project Coordination: Editorial Directions, Inc.
Photo Research: Alice K. Flanagan

**Library of Congress Cataloging-in-Publication Data**
Klingel, Cynthia Fitterer.
Farmers / by Cynthia Klingel and Robert B. Noyed.
    p. cm.
ISBN 1-56766-940-9 (lib. bdg : alk. paper)
1. Agriculture—Juvenile literature.  2. Farmers—Juvenile literature.
[1. Farmers. 2. Farm life. 3. Occupations.]    I. Noyed, Robert B. II. Title.
S519 .K53 2001
630'.92'2—dc21
                                    2001000791